NICK
GOES TO
VEGAS – ALONE

By

Karen Weller

DEDICATION

To my late sister, Sarah Felicity Strawson, whose imagination soared higher than a giraffe's and whose determination was as mighty as an elephant's. She built worlds from her dreams and brought them to life with a magic all her own.

INTRODUCTION

Nothing – not a word. Did he get there ok? Did he lose his phone? Please don't tell me he was mugged at the airport for his phone!

All these thoughts went through my head. He always texted or spoke to me every couple of hours if he went away. Alright, it was normally a Veterinary convention, not a weekend away with the boys, but really, was I that unforgettable?

I sent the 30th text since he left, and although it was only a couple of hours flight, I was starting to get worried now, and Kiki was pacing, so I'm not sure if she knew or just sensed my anxiety.

Melissa had been absent for several days, so I can only presume we will have another thousand baby spiders ready to hatch shortly. I really hope she hasn't made the nest in my slipper again; that was enough to make me recoil in horror last time.

Wait, the phone is ringing…

CHAPTER 1:
NICK GETS AN INVITE

How do I broach the subject?

"Excuse me, love — do you mind if I go on a bit of a bender for Steve's stag do? The boys will meet me there, so no worries. I won't drink much, and I'll text you all the time."

Not exactly reassuring. I needed to think of something else to say.

Maybe: "Hey, love. I just fancy a couple of nights gambling in Las Vegas. Figured you and Chloe wouldn't want to come, so I've booked a single room."

Nope. That sounded even worse.

"Hey, babe, I know you've been away—"

No, that wouldn't work either, especially since the trip to her parents' place went so wrong when Chloe got abducted by her brother-in-law.

Maybe I should just tell her the truth: it'll be raucous, there'll be alcohol, and I'll be back on Monday.

Yes, just be honest, so I was. I did not expect the silent treatment all day, though.

Was it that bad that I wanted some time to talk about non-baby stuff? I loved Chloe dearly, but was losing myself in the world as all our married friends just want to come and hold the baby – what happened to boys' nights with a beer and a game of cards?

So, off I went to tell her, not ask her, that I was going.

'Morning, beautiful. How are you doing this morning? You are looking amazingly stunning this morning,' I said.

'What are you after, Nick? I look and feel like 100 years old since I had Chloe, so whatever you want, just ask me before I go back to sleep when Chloe has her nap.'

Wow, this was not going to be easy. I already felt like a drag to even think of going away and leaving them, but I hadn't had a weekend off since Chloe was born, as Sarah would normally cover the Saturday shift, but since we had Chloe, she was just too tired to see lots of clients and their animals.

'I wanted to go to Vegas on Friday as Steve is having a two-night bachelor party, you know, a few drinks, small gambling – nothing outrageous,' I said, not really believing anything I was saying. Sarah had never questioned my spending, not that I spent anything except on the animals, Kiki, Melissa (who names and gets attached to a spider?), and any poor little orphan that Sarah takes in rather than leave in the surgery overnight.

'That would be good for you, you deserve to let off some steam as you work so hard,' said Sarah. Wow, that was easy. As I heard her go back in the bedroom, I was sure she would realise what I had said and come stomping back out again.

No, all was well, and during tea I mentioned it again, and she said she would sort out some cover in case any client's animals got sick, as she couldn't manage Chloe and the practice.

So it was, I was off to Vegas and so excited, I couldn't sleep for the next three nights.

CAESARS PALACE
BELLAGIO
CAESARS PALACE
VENETIAN
Exc

CHAPTER 2:
VEGAS

Whoa, this palace is awesome. Straight from the plane, a limo picked the three of us up and took us to Caesars Palace. The room was stunning, more like a suite really, and the champagne on ice went down a bit too well on an empty stomach.

By the time we went down to the casino, we were all quite merry, so we went straight to the food hall and had a snack. If anyone has been to America, they will know the snacks are bigger than the main meals.

We hit the tables soon after, and very quickly, I had lost about $500, so I reigned myself in; otherwise, my budget wouldn't last the weekend. Steve was having a blast on the craps table; he had quite a stash of chips in front of him, and it wasn't long before a crowd had gathered to watch him. Guess they would have been happy if he lost it all, too, as jealousy doesn't really exist in Vegas, so win or lose, he was on a roll.

By this point, the third member of our party had gone off with a lady dressed in red, so we didn't expect to see him again all weekend.

I stayed and watched Steve for a while, then walked to some slot machines where I could gamble 88 cents at a time, much more in line with my budget.

I was winning quite a bit and kept cashing out the ticket every time I won more than my original bet, then putting the equivalent of my original bet back in again until I won. After about an hour or so, I had no idea what time it was, as there were no clocks or natural daylight in the casinos. I went to the craps table, but Steve had gone. You can't talk to the croupier, so I asked a couple of people if they had seen Steve, and they said no, they didn't remember anyone winning that volume of chips.

I thought this was strange, as I am sure some of them were there when he was. I went walking round the casino floor, bear in mind it is about half a mile square, so it took some time, but there was no sign of Steve, so I went back to the room to check on him.

I couldn't find my room key, so I had to go back to the reception and was baffled when they said I hadn't checked in. I enquired about Steve and his friend, but they said they had no record of us there. I could clearly recall us all standing there, like a bunch of schoolboys again.

WHAT WAS HAPPENING? I HAD DOLLARS IN MY POCKET, SOME WINNING TICKETS, MY BODY FELT FULL OF ADRENALINE AND ALCOHOL (NOT A GREAT MIX), AND NO STEVE.

I WENT BACK TO THE ROOM AND BANGED ON THE DOOR, AND A YOUNG, WEALTHY-LOOKING GUY ANSWERED, NOT SOMEONE I HAD SEEN BEFORE. HE OOZED WEALTH AND WAS DRIPPING IN GOLD BRACELETS AND CHAINS, THE SORT OF PERSON YOU WOULD THINK COULD AFFORD THIS SUITE, UNLIKE MY FRIENDS AND ME.

I EXPLAINED WHAT I COULD TO HIM, AND HE SAID THAT THEY HAD BEEN IN THE ROOM FOR 3 DAYS, AND HE LET ME IN TO LOOK FOR MY BAG WITH A VERY PUZZLED LOOK ON HIS FACE. WHERE WERE OUR BAGS, WHERE WAS MY JACKET, AND WHERE WERE MY FRIENDS? I WAS NOW BEGINNING TO FREAK OUT A LITTLE.

I LEFT THE ROOM AND WENT BACK TO THE FRONT DESK, NOT SURE EXACTLY WHAT I WAS GOING TO ASK THEM.

CHAPTER 3:
SARAH AND CHLOE
TAKE A TRIP

This was scary; not only could I not get hold of Nick, but his friend Steve's phone, which Nick had given me the number for, was also turned off.

Kiki came over and asked if she could do anything. I told her what was going on, and she sat quietly for a moment.

'I can't visualise Nick. He is normally quite clear to me because of his connection to you, Sarah,' Kiki said (or rather, my Guardian Angel called Felicity, who was able to jump between any of my animals, it seemed). Now I started to panic. What had happened?

I phoned the airline, which confirmed their plane had arrived safely and also that Nick was a passenger on that flight. I knew I had to go there, go to Vegas, but how and what about Chloe?

Two hours later, and I was packed with enough clothes for myself and Chloe for the journey. After all, we should be back tomorrow. Once I find Nick, I will drag him home on the next flight. Really, he had told me not to worry, it was just a couple of days with the boys, and he would be home; well, he would be home because I would make him come home.

AND SO IT WAS, THE PLANE TOOK OFF, AND CHLOE AND I JUST SNUGGLED FOR THE COUPLE OF HOURS, AND WHEN WE LANDED, SHE WAS FAST ASLEEP, WHICH WAS GOOD AS IT GOT ME THROUGH BORDER CONTROL A LOT QUICKER.

I SET FOOT OUTSIDE AND HEADED FOR THE CAB RANK. WITH A CHILD IN TOW, I WAS NOT GOING TO GET A SHUTTLE BUS.

I TOLD THE DRIVER TO GO TO CAESARS PALACE, AS NICK HAD SAID THAT WAS WHERE THEY WERE STAYING. WHEN WE GOT THERE, I COULD FEEL MELISSA WAS WITH ME AGAIN; SHE HAD POPPED UP ON MY ARM AS IF BY MAGIC, BUT I KNEW KIKI HAD SENT HER. SHE WAS ON HIGH ALERT AS SHE TOLD ME SHE FELT SOMETHING WAS WRONG. WELL, I KNEW THAT, OR I WOULDN'T HAVE BEEN HERE, WOULD I?

I WENT TO THE RECEPTION AS I HAD PUT CHLOE IN HER STROLLER NOW, AND THE LADY THERE TOLD ME THEY HAD NOBODY BOOKED IN UNDER NICK'S OR STEVE'S NAME. THAT CAN'T BE RIGHT, SO I ASKED HER TO CHECK AGAIN. STILL THE SAME. MELISSA THEN BIT ME, AS MUCH AS A NON–VENOMOUS SPIDER CAN DO, AND I FLEW MY HEAD ROUND TO SEE NICK SITTING IN ONE OF THE RECEPTION CHAIRS. I RAN TO HIM, AND HIS FACE LIT UP TO SEE ME, BUT THEN HE SAID, 'WHAT ARE YOU DOING HERE? I CAN'T FIND STEVE, AND THE RECEPTIONIST TOLD ME WE NEVER BOOKED IN.'

I HUGGED HIM SO TIGHTLY AS HIS WHOLE BODY SHOOK WITH RELIEF AT SEEING SOMEONE HE KNEW. HE LOOKED SO LONELY THAT I DIDN'T WANT TO LET HIM GO. IT WAS SO SAD THAT SOMETHING COULD HAVE GONE WRONG WITH HIS FEW DAYS AWAY CELEBRATING WITH HIS FRIEND.

WE SAT DOWN, AND AS HE HELD CHLOE, WHO WAS DELIGHTED TO SEE HIM, WE CHATTED MORE, AND HE TOLD ME ABOUT HIS GAMBLING AND STEVE WINNING LOADS. AND THEN, HE TOLD ME ABOUT STEVE DISAPPEARING INTO THIN AIR.

OK, THIS ALL SOUNDED VERY STRANGE, SO HE CHECKED HIS BANK BALANCE, AND IT WAS FINE. WE MANAGED TO BOOK AN AIRBNB FOR THE NIGHT, AND ONCE IN THERE, HE JUST BROKE DOWN IN TEARS, NOT SURE IF HE HAD DREAMED THE WHOLE THING.

I ASKED HIM TO LOOK IN HIS POCKETS, AND YES, THE WINNING SLOT MACHINE TICKETS WERE ALL THERE. HE HAD WON JUST OVER $1,000, SO HE HAD MADE A PROFIT. I TOLD HIM WE WOULD GO AND CASH THEM IN AT CAESARS TOMORROW.

HE TOLD ME HE REMEMBERS GETTING IN THE LIMO, COMING TO THE CASINO, SEEING STEVE WIN, AND THEN EVERYTHING CHANGED.

WE WENT TO BED AND CHATTED SOME MORE, AND THE NEXT MORNING WE WENT TO A PHARMACY AND HAD SOME BLOOD TESTS DONE TO SEE WHAT MIGHT HAVE HAPPENED.

LO AND BEHOLD, THE TESTS SHOWED THAT HIS DRINK HAD BEEN SPIKED ABOUT 5 MINUTES AFTER LANDING, SO IT MUST HAVE BEEN IN THE LIMO. NO WONDER HE COULDN'T REMEMBER ANYTHING. NICK NOW DISPLAYED ANGER AT THE SITUATION, KNOWING HE WASN'T GOING CRAZY (I AM SURE HE THOUGHT HE WAS HAVING A MIDLIFE CRISIS IN HIS 20'S).

MELISSA WAS NOW BITING THE BACK OF MY HAND AND SOFTLY SAID, JUST TO ME, THAT SHE THINKS WE NEED TO GO TO THE LIMO CONTRACTORS FOR SOME ANSWERS.

GREAT IDEA, AND I RELAYED THIS TO STEVE, WHO SAID WE WOULD GO ONCE HE HAD MORE COFFEE.

CASINO
CASINO
CASINO
777
777
777

Chapter 4:
Nick and Steve

I WENT TO THE HATCH WHERE THE LIMO CONTRACTORS WERE BASED AND TOLD THEM THE TIME AND LOCATION OF THE LIMO WE HAD BOOKED. WHEN THEY SAID THEY WOULD HAVE A RECORDING OF THE INSIDE OF THE LIMO, I WAS SO HAPPY THAT THIS WHOLE THING WOULD BE OVER QUICKLY.
WE SAT AND WATCHED THE RECORDING. IT WAS OBVIOUS WE WERE ALL THERE, BUT WAIT, WHAT WAS STEVE'S FRIEND DOING? HE HAD TOLD US TO TAKE SOME VIDEO FOOTAGE, SO AS WE DROVE DOWN THE STRIP OF CASINOS, STEVE AND I HAD BEEN STANDING WITH OUR HEADS THROUGH THE SUNROOF OF THE LIMO. WITH CLOSER EXAMINATION, I COULD SEE HIS FRIEND PUT SOMETHING IN OUR DRINKS, BUT NOT HIS OWN. WHAT ON EARTH WAS GOING ON?
I WATCHED SOME MORE, BUT IT JUST SHOWED STEVE AND ME ASLEEP FOR THE NEXT TWENTY MINUTES, AND THEN HIS FRIEND WAS MANHANDLING US OUT OF THE LIMO.
OK, SO WHAT NOW? I THOUGHT.
SARAH HAD JUST COME BACK FROM A WALK WITH THE STROLLER, AND, WITH CHLOE FAST ASLEEP, WE THOUGHT THROUGH OUR OPTIONS.

1. DO NOTHING AND GO HOME TOMORROW AS PLANNED.
2. LOOK FOR STEVE.

OBVIOUSLY, THE SECOND OPTION WAS THE ONLY ONE, AS HE HAD BEEN MY FRIEND SINCE HIGH SCHOOL.

IT WAS NOW ABOUT 2 O'CLOCK, AND IT WAS HOT HERE, SO WE TOOK CHLOE AND WENT FOR COLD DRINKS WHILE WE THOUGHT THIS THROUGH. SARAH MUST HAVE HAD QUITE AN ITCH AS SHE KEPT SHAKING HER LEFT HAND; MAYBE SHE HAD BEEN BITTEN BY A MOSQUITO OR SOMETHING.

SUDDENLY, SARAH SAID SHE THOUGHT WE SHOULD GO BACK TO THE LIMO CONTRACTORS AND LOOK AROUND TO SEE IF WE COULD FIND OUT WHO THIS FRIEND OF STEVE'S WAS.

I WONDERED WHAT SHE THOUGHT WE WOULD FIND OUT, BUT WENT ALONG WITH IT ANYWAY.

AS WE APPROACHED THE LIMO COMPANY AGAIN, I THOUGHT I RECOGNISED A GUY IN A FLAT CAP WALKING AWAY, SO I SPRINTED AFTER HIM AND CAUGHT HOLD OF HIS SLEEVE AS HE STARTED TO RUN AWAY. 'HEY, WHAT'S GOING ON, WHERE'S STEVE?' I ASKED HIM. HE JUST SHOOK HIS HEAD AND LOOKED LIKE HE WANTED TO RUN AWAY. HE RELUCTANTLY SAID HE HAD KNOWN STEVE FOR SEVERAL YEARS, AND STEVE HAD RUN UP DEBTS IN VEGAS AND OWED MONEY TO THE LOCAL MOB, NOT THE SAME AS THE OLD MOB, WHO WOULD HAVE TAKEN HIM TO THE DESERT AND LEFT HIM BURIED IN THE SAND FOR THE BIRDS TO PECK AT.

Well, that was news to me, so I asked how much he owed. The guy said about $50,000, and with daily interest, it was now about $70,000. I couldn't speak; this was about my mate Steve. So eventually, with a deep breath, I asked him why I thought I had been in the casino. He said it was the powder he put in our drinks, which makes you think what you want to do. So, as I was happy to be here, it made me think nice thoughts, like Steve winning. I had gotten the winning machine tickets, so how did they end up if it wasn't real? He said they had put them in my pocket while I was sleeping to make me think it was all ok.

Gosh, this was a bit unreal, and my head was spinning with how clever the whole setup had been.

He told me about the mob, well, one guy really, who owned most of the gambling debts, had Steve at his house, locked in the garage, and was holding him for ransom from his wife, since they knew they owned and had paid for their house, which was worth nearly $1,000,000.00. I knew their house was big but hadn't seen it, so I had no idea of its value.

Sarah was listening to all of this intently, like she was conjuring up a plan in her head, at the same time as feeding Chloe. Wait, what? Did I just see a spider walk on her hand? I went to swat it away, but it had already run up her sleeve. Sarah didn't seem phased by this and just said to leave it as she didn't want to drop Chloe or something – very weird as I am sure she told me when we met, she didn't want to treat any spiders in the surgery as she was terrified of them.

I asked the guy where this mobster lived, and he told me, but said not to go near his house as he was very dangerous. I started to think Sarah had other ideas by the look on her face.

I let the guy go, seriously hoping we would never see him again, as he had turned out to be no friend of Steve's, just a lackey for the mob man to get his money back.

Sarah looked up at me and smiled. She said we were taking a ride, and I reminded her we had a child in tow, to which she replied that she knew that.

GRAND LOBBY · CASINO ENTRANCE
HOTEL DIRECTORY

CHAPTER 5: SARAH HATCHES HER PLAN

It was getting dusk now, and the temperature was falling, but who knew my friend from California just happened to be at a convention in Vegas this weekend. I rang her and asked if she could look after Chloe for a few hours. She was delighted, and we met her in Denny's, where we bought her a supper, and then parted ways after seeing her address, where she was staying, to collect Chloe later.

Nick and I set off, not really knowing where we were going in a cab, but Uber, being Uber, used satnav all the time, so it got us to the end of the street where we needed to be, and we parted ways. I didn't want the driver knowing which house we had gone to, just in case things took a turn for the worse. Melissa had also told me that we were getting nearer to Steve and that the house was empty, so now would be a good time. I knew I couldn't tell Nick how I knew this information, so I just said it was a hunch. I know sometimes he thinks I am psychic or something, but if I told him my animals spoke to me, he would just leave me and say I am cuckoo.

So, we walked to the garage, and an external light shone brightly with our movements; it was so bright that I wish I had brought shades for my eyes. A mobster would want an early warning system, I was sure. We got to the garage door and could hear music, only quietly, but still it was music. Nick shouted Steve's name, but there was no reply. I hoped they hadn't hurt him, as, although he obviously owed them pots of money, deep down he came across as a lovely family guy, and I was sure they could have worked something out.

I tried the handle, and the door opened, but my biggest surprise was when we went in, the main light turned on, and Steve was hunched over an old Ford Cadillac; he appeared to be working on it. I went straight to him and thumped him on the back as the music was louder in here. He turned, surprised to see us. I knew, I knew right then that we had been lied to, that Steve was the house owner, and he had made up the story about owing money to get rid of his friend. Nick turned the radio off and stomped over, looking angry.

'What is going on, Steve? We thought we would have to rescue you if you weren't already, you know, dead?' said Nick.

Steve just looked at him, hung his head in shame, and told us the story.

Many years ago, he met his friend, the one in the car with them, and he had borrowed some money to put a deposit on their house back in Tennessee. He hadn't been able to make the repayments in the last six months, so he concocted a story about owing gambling debts to the mobster. His friend had sucked all this in, not knowing that Steve was wealthy, so wealthy on paper, but his house here and at home were both mortgaged to the brim from real gambling debt. Steve said his wife didn't know, so he had made up the story to get his parents-in-law to give them some money so he could gamble it and maybe win more (again, don't gamble, guys, it's not worth it). Oh, I was so angry now, and that explained why Melissa had told me no bad people were at home, as she had only sensed Steve, who wasn't a threat to Nick or me. I walked out of the garage and made a call to my friend who had Chloe. I asked her to keep her for the night, as she had a supply of diapers in the bag I gave her. She was very happy to have her sleepover with Chloe.

Nick and I took Steve into the house and sat with him while he produced papers showing what he owed on both houses.

I said it would make sense for him to sell the one we were currently sitting in and for him to never return to Vegas again. He nodded his head, saying how wise I was and how sorry he was for all the trouble he had caused. Nick looked at me and said he would go with Steve to the realtor (estate agent) tomorrow and get the house valued. It should be enough to clear the debt here, and then when we were back in Tennessee, he would go with Steve to the bank to sort that house out. Steve must have been a great mate to Nick at school, as this was further than I would have gone for one of my girlfriends.

We took Steve with us so he couldn't get into any more trouble until Nick helped him tomorrow and stopped at a diner to eat again (it really is all I have done since leaving England – eat). While we ate, Steve seemed to be a lot happier, and he had brought his personal belongings from the house. We had tidied up as well, so all the agent would need to do was go in and take photos and advertise an open day for folk to go and look around in the interest of buying the house.

After the food, we hit the Airbnb and sat talking, and I checked in with my friend to see if Chloe was doing OK, and we said I would collect her at 9 am the following morning.

We rose early and again headed to a diner for breakfast, and then Steve and Nick set off to the realtor to sort out the house sale.

I collected Chloe and my friend, Melissa, and we went to the park. Chloe would never know that the spider came too, but Melissa had a whale of a time on the back of Chloe's jumper, being held, going down a baby slide. Maybe this is the perfect world, but if it isn't, it sure does come close.

At about 1 o'clock, we set off to meet Nick and make our way to the airport, Melissa was chatting away to me but obviously once we met Nick I couldn't answer her (weird person talking to a spider – not a great look), so I listened while she told me the texts on Nicks phone read that Steve had signed the house over to the realtor and now it would be good that he flew back to Tennessee with us to see his wife and come clean. Nick had replied that he would go with him as support.

It was handy having a text reader, but I did feel like I was spying on Nick by knowing his texts, so I told Melissa, in very quiet whispers, not to tell me unless it impacted Chloe or me. The day rolled into the flight time, and as I settled with Nick and Chloe on the plane, I felt the weight of the last few days slip away. It had been an experience, but why don't adults talk to each other like children do? If something is wrong, then chat it out. Two heads are better than one, as the saying goes.

We arrived home about 8 in the evening, and Nick went straight to the surgery next door to check on everything while Chloe, Melissa, and I went to see Kiki, who had been visited three times a day to maintain her diet and exercise regimen while we were away.

Kiki was so excited that she clambered all over me within seconds. Felicity had moved from within Melissa to Kiki. While Kiki was telling me how much Felicity had enjoyed her slide and playpark adventure, she asked why she hadn't been able to go.

I EXPLAINED TO KIKI, THEN STOPPED MYSELF FROM CHATTING MORE AS I REALISED SHE WAS SMILING BECAUSE, OF COURSE, IT WAS FELICITY TALKING AND SHE HAD BEEN WITH US ALL THE TIME INSIDE MELISSA, SO KIKI WAS JUST BEING CHEEKY, MAKING OUT SHE KNEW NOTHING OF OUR ADVENTURE. I REALLY NEEDED MY BED, AND FOR THAT NIGHT ONLY, SO I ALLOWED KIKI TO SLEEP WITH US; NORMALLY, HER BODY TEMPERATURE RUNS TOO HIGH, AND SHE IS LIKE A HOT WATER BOTTLE, BUT I HAD REALLY MISSED HER. NICK HAD MISSED HER, TOO, BUT HE WOULD NEVER LET HER KNOW THAT. AS SHE CURLED HER LEFT HAND AROUND HIS NECK, I HEARD HIM SIGH AND TELL HER HE LOVED HER BEFORE HE DRIFTED OFF TO SLEEP. I WISH I HAD RECORDED THAT, AS I WOULD HAVE TEASED HIM IN THE MORNING.

STEVE'S AUTO
STEVE'S WORKSHOP
— EST 1970 —
7:30 PM

CHAPTER 5: MELISSA MAKES SENSE OF IT ALL

WHY DO HUMANS NEED SO MUCH LOOKING AFTER? I HAD NEARLY BITTEN MY TEETH DOWN TO THE GUMS WITH THE AMOUNT OF TRYING TO GET SARAH'S ATTENTION; HER SKIN LOOKED SO SILKY, BUT HAD WEATHERED SO MUCH BY SEEING FARM ANIMALS SINCE SHE CAME TO THIS SURGERY (HER WORDS, NOT MINE).

SHE NEARLY FORGOT AT ONE POINT THAT I WAS IN HER POCKET AND SHOVED HER PHONE IN WITH ME. THAT HURT AS IT HIT ME RIGHT ON MY NOSE, AND MY NOSE IS TINY, SO GOOD SHOT, SARAH!

I KNOW HUMANS TRY TO HELP HUMANS, BUT BOY, THEY DO GET IN SOME FIXES. WHY CAN'T THEIR LIFE BE SIMPLE LIKE MINE? HAVE SOME BABIES, WAIT FOR THEM TO HATCH, THEN SHOW THEM THE DOOR, EAT, AND REPEAT. WOW, LIFE WAS PERFECT, I THINK I WILL STAY HOME NEXT TIME, TRAVELLING IS NOT FOR ME AT ALL.

I WOULD BE GLAD TO GO HOME. IT IS SO WEIRD TO HAVE A SPIRIT INSIDE ME GUIDING SARAH. I DON'T KNOW HOW KIKI CONTROLS THE SPIRIT, AS I FIND IT SO ANNOYING WHEN IT KEEPS PROMPTING ME TO GET HER ATTENTION. I FEEL THIS SORT OF HAND GRAB MY INSIDES, SO I BITE SARAH, AND THEN THE SPIRIT TALKS. SARAH DOESN'T REALLY THINK IT'S ME TALKING, DOES SHE?

IF I HAD SOME FOOD FOR EVERY TIME I FEEL NAUSEOUS FROM THE SPIRIT, I WOULD BE SO ROUND IT WOULD BE DIFFICULT FOR ME TO MOVE. MAYBE WHEN WE GET HOME, KIKI WILL KEEP FELICITY, AND I WON'T BE IN THIS POSITION AGAIN. ALTHOUGH I DON'T KNOW HOW KIKI COULD TRAVEL WITH SARAH, AS SHE IS A BIT LARGE AND ALL ARMS AND LEGS, MAYBE I WILL NEED TO GO AND HELP THE NEXT TIME AROUND, WHO KNOWS.

THE END